ANNIKA,
The Queen of Light

ANNIKA,
The Queen of Light

AND OTHER STORIES OF
CHILDREN AROUND THE WORLD
Compiled by the Editors
of
Highlights for Children

CONTENTS

ANNIKA,
The Queen of Light

By Judy Cox

Annika sat on the bed and watched Kerstin fold the last sweater and pack it neatly into her big gray suitcase. "I wish you weren't going," Annika told her big sister. "College seems so grown up. Next thing you know, you'll be getting married and moving out completely."

Kerstin laughed, the merry sound that was so much a part of Annika's home. "Silly, Annika! That's years and years away. And I'll be home for Christmas." She shut the lid of her suitcase and zipped it up. "Christmas! That reminds me. Annika, you'll have to be Lucia this year. My vacation won't start in time." It was the custom in Sweden for the oldest girl to wake her family on St. Lucia's Day, wearing a crown of lit candles and carrying a tray of coffee and buns.

"Oh, no! I can't be Lucia!" cried Annika. "Kerstin, can't you come home sooner? You've always been Lucia." Annika thought of Kerstin, tall, blond, graceful Kerstin, dressed all in white with a crown glowing on her head like a living Christmas tree. Kerstin looked like a Queen of Light.

Annika surveyed her short, stocky body and straight brown hair in Kerstin's mirror. She, on the other hand, didn't look like a queen. *I look more like* Jultomtar, *the little Christmas troll,* she thought.

Kerstin laughed again and picked up her heavy suitcases. "No, I can't come home sooner. Don't worry so much, Annika, you'll make a wonderful Lucia!" A car horn honked outside. "Helga's here! Here, you can carry this downstairs for me." Kerstin handed Annika a suitcase.

Annika waved until Helga's car was out of sight. Then she sighed. *It'll be forever until Kerstin comes home again,* she thought.

But the weeks flew by. The leaves brightened to gold and then turned brown and fell, soft as snowflakes. Soon the snow covered the ground. Before long, it was December 12, the day before St. Lucia's Day.

"Hold still, Annika!" ordered Mama. "It's like trying to pin a wave." Annika tried to stand still as Mama pinned up her new white dress. "It's a shame this dress was too long," Mama said. "I'll hem it tonight." Mama took the last pin out of her mouth.

"Will I be all right?" asked Annika anxiously. She remembered Kerstin's polished gracefulness. *I will never be able to balance the wreath of lit candles on my head and carry the heavy tray all the way upstairs without spilling something,* Annika thought.

"You'll be just fine, dear," said Mama. "Now, it's time to make the Lucia buns." They went into the kitchen to make the saffron-flavored buns.

"What if I drop the tray, Mama?" Annika asked anxiously, as she kneaded the dough.

Mama laughed, but the sound was kind. "You will not drop the tray, dear. You will hold your head up high and proud, for you will be the Queen of Light, letting us know that winter will soon end and the long days return." When the dough had risen, Mama showed Annika how to roll it into little snakes, and coil them around. Annika made some into little cat faces, with raisins for eyes.

9

That night, she could hardly close her eyes because of her excitement. But the house was dark and quiet, and Annika's bed warm, and somehow she fell asleep in spite of herself.

It was still dark outside when she heard the cuckoo clock sing the hour. Six cuckoos. St. Lucia's Day! The wood floor was cold on her bare feet. She shivered as she pulled on her white dress and tied the red sash. She stood before Kerstin's mirror and brushed her hair one hundred strokes to make it shine.

Downstairs, she carefully set the tray with cups and saucers and the plate of buns. She poured coffee and hot chocolate into little pots. Then she put on the Lucia crown that Mama had made, anchoring it firmly with hairpins. The crown was made of twisted whortleberry leaves and held six tall, white candles. With trembling fingers she lit the candles, watching her reflection in the dark kitchen window. She stood a moment, caught by the vision of her own face surrounded by candle flames. *I do look like the Queen of Light!* she thought. At last, breathing a sigh of determination, she lifted the tray.

Steadily, trying to glide as smoothly as she'd seen Kerstin do, Annika carried the tray upstairs. The stairs were dark, lit only by the flickering golden glow of the candles in her crown. She went upstairs slowly, her head held high, singing the Lucia song. Suddenly her foot became tangled in a loose bit of hem. She stumbled. The tray tilted toward the floor, the pile of buns slipping . . .

Annika caught herself and stood up straight. A close call. Carefully, she walked down the hall to her parents' room.

Still singing, she set the tray down on the small table near the bed.

"Good morning, Annika—I mean Lucia!" called her father, sitting up. He waited patiently while Annika poured out the coffee, spilling not a single drop on the white counterpane.

When Annika was finished serving the buns and coffee, Mama leaned over and blew out the candles on her wreath with a single breath. "We know you are the Queen of Light," said Mama. "And very nice you look, indeed. But no use taking any chances, is there?"

Annika gave a sigh of perfect contentment. She'd done it! It was nice to be finished with the worry of the lit crown, but she would forever remember the feeling of being surrounded by its warm glow. She sat on the edge of the bed and munched her Lucia cat bun and sipped her hot chocolate. Next week, Kerstin would be home. Annika couldn't wait to tell her all about it!

The Sea Watcher

By Peter Roop

Thorfinn watched the eagle soar higher and higher. Then, as swift as an arrow, it fell, catching its prey in midflight.

"Over there," Thorfinn said, pointing. "High above the Sea Watcher's Rock."

"I can barely see the Rock, much less an eagle above it," complained Eric. "Thorfinn, your eyes are better than the eagle's. You can see farther than anyone in the village."

Thorfinn turned and looked at his older brother.

"Then why won't they let me watch for Father's ship?" he asked.

"You know why," Eric replied. "Only the captain's eldest son can be the Sea Watcher."

"Even though he can't see well enough to find the eagle," Thorfinn said in disgust.

Eric sighed. "Come on," he said. "I'll race you home. Last one there must clean all the fish."

The brothers raced along the beach to the Viking village, sand flying beneath their bare feet. They arrived, breathless and laughing, at their stone hut. Thorfinn won the race by a yard.

He lifted the rough hide that covered the hut's entrance. His mother was rolling out dough, her strong hands kneading it smooth. Grandfather sat by the fire. His hands were as knotted as the fishnet he was mending.

"I see your luck continues," Mother said as the brothers held up their dripping fish. "Whose turn is it to clean them?"

Thorfinn smiled and handed his fish to Eric, who went outside to scrape them. Thorfinn drew close to the fire. Several times he almost turned to Grandfather with the question that burned as hot inside him as the dancing flames.

"The fisherman looks sad," said Grandfather. "Maybe he took too many fish from their homes?"

"No, Grandfather. Fishing doesn't make me sad," Thorfinn said. Then his thoughts slipped out. "Why must the eldest son be the only one allowed to watch for Father's ship? Why not the one with the best eyes?"

Grandfather sighed. "Why, you ask. Why, I cannot tell you. It has always been done that way. It will always be, until someone proves that a new way is better."

That night Thorfinn lay awake. The ship and its crew had been gone a month longer than his father had said they would be. This was the stormy season, and already several bad storms had come. Thorfinn wished his father were home safely, sleeping in the hut with the family.

Thorfinn tossed and turned under the warm sealskin. The night was still. No wind blew in from the ocean. He heard the shepherd's dog bark on a faraway hillside. Then, like a fresh breeze filling a limp sail, there came an idea.

Thorfinn got up with the sun. He put a long loaf of fresh bread into his bag and crept silently to Grandfather's bedside. The older man was already awake.

"I'm going to the hill to help Johan with the sheep," Thorfinn whispered. "Please tell Mother I will return in a few days."

Grandfather nodded his white head. His smile told Thorfinn that he understood the plan.

Far away on the hill Thorfinn saw small white dots he knew to be Johan's sheep. As he drew closer, he called, "Johan! May I visit you for a few days?"

"You are most welcome at my rocky home," Johan replied.

Inside the small shelter, the boys sat by a blazing fire, talking about the village and eating dried fish and Thorfinn's bread. Through the shepherd's open door, Thorfinn saw the wide ocean stretching westward to the edge of the world. Somewhere out there was his father.

All day the boys herded the hungry sheep to fresh grass. The eastern ocean was hidden by the steep ridge behind them. But Thorfinn's eyes often slipped to the western horizon, to search for the sail of a returning ship.

That night several of the sheep wandered over the ridge. In the morning Johan sent Thorfinn to drive them back.

Thorfinn climbed to the top of the ridge. The sea unfolded around the entire island in every direction. Searching the western waters, his sharp eyes found no sail. Then, turning eastward to look for the lost sheep, he caught the glimmer of something moving upon the water.

A ship? he thought hopefully. *No. Father will be coming from the west, not the east.*

Thorfinn squinted against the sun until his eyes ached. Then once more he saw it—a ship, but one with no sail. It was disabled, rocking sideways upon the ocean swells.

Forgetting the sheep, Thorfinn dashed down the hill, flashing past an astonished Johan. He raced into the village. "A ship!" he cried. "I saw a ship on the eastern waters!"

Women and children poured from their huts. Fishermen on shore pushed Thorfinn into a fishing boat, and he pointed the way to the disabled ship. As they approached, Thorfinn could see the weary faces of the crew. His father gripped the tiller weakly.

The fishing boat pulled alongside the ship. Thorfinn threw a long rope to his father, and the damaged craft was towed safely into harbor.

Later, after a rest, Thorfinn's father gathered the villagers together to tell of the voyage.

"Gusting winds forced us off course and shredded our sails, snapping the mast off as if it were rotten wood," he said. "We sailed completely past the island. For days we rowed back, our food and water gone. Then yesterday we spotted the island, but we were too weak to row. If it hadn't been for

Thorfinn's sharp eyes, no one would have spotted us until it was too late."

He gave Thorfinn a tired smile and tousled his hair. Then he continued in a stronger voice.

"For as long as the village can remember, the Sea Watcher has been the captain's eldest son. Our ship's misfortune has shown the folly of such a tradition. Let it be decided that the Sea Watcher will be the one with the best eyes. Our new Sea Watcher is Thorfinn."

The villagers cheered, and Eric clapped his brother on the back. With his eagle eyes, Thorfinn would make a fine Sea Watcher. And one day, when they were old enough, he and Eric would join their father on the sea.

The Olive Tree

By Elsa Marston

The stone house next door had stood empty for a long time. Saleem did not remember the family who owned it, for they had left before he was born.

Saleem's homeland of Lebanon had been torn by years of conflict among people of different religions. Some, like the Besharas, had moved away from homes where they had formerly lived in peace with their neighbors. Now, thank goodness, the Besharas were coming back. As Saleem watched them carrying in mattresses, cooking pots, and suitcases, he hoped they would have a boy about his age.

He also wondered about the large old olive tree in the Besharas' yard. It produced the best olives in Lebanon, his mother always said as she put them up in jars with lemon and hot pepper. Saleem's family had enjoyed those olives for as long as he could remember. Would that change?

The Beshara family soon settled in their house. They were always polite to their neighbors, but they did not return the visits or the hospitable gifts such as fresh figs and plates of stuffed vine leaves. Saleem heard his parents say the Besharas still seemed uneasy. And what was more, they did not have a boy. They had a girl named Nada who wanted nothing to do with Saleem.

No one said anything about the fine old olive tree, and Saleem wondered when they would.

Soon the plump green olives started to ripen. They dropped to the ground and, as always, Saleem gathered them up.

One morning he noticed Nada leaning on the rocky wall between their two yards. For a while she watched without saying anything. And then she spoke.

"Those are our olives. Ours!"

Saleem straightened up to face her. "They're on our land."

"Yes, but the *tree* is on *our* land," Nada said. "It grows in our soil, its roots go under our house, it drinks our water. It has belonged to my family for a hundred years."

Yes, as Saleem knew very well, the tree belonged to the Besharas. But it is the nature of olive trees, as they grow older, to twist into strange, contorted shapes. While the trunk of the Besharas' tree stood firmly on their land, many of the large limbs stretched far over the wall. They dropped the best olives in Lebanon onto the property of Saleem's family.

Saleem said, "All the time you were away, we took care of this tree. We pruned it and watered it. We have a right to the olives."

"But now we're back, and we'll take care of it!" said Nada. "My father will see to it that we get the olives."

Saleem dumped all the olives he had gathered on the ground and stalked away. For a few days, the fruit went on dropping and simply lay there in the dust.

One night a fierce storm rolled over the mountains. Thunder boomed and lightning flashed. One terrible bolt seemed to shake the whole world. At daybreak Saleem rushed outside.

The olive tree was gone. Its beautiful silvery-green leaves were blown far and wide, and the tree lay in lumps and splinters, scattered over the yards of the two families. Nada and her family stood on their side of the wall, which had also been broken when the lightning struck. Saleem and his family stood on their side.

Everyone stared at what was left of the tree. Then, one by one, the grown-ups drifted sadly back into their houses.

Saleem remained, his large, dark eyes threatening to spill their tears. No more shade from the comforting branches with their softly whispering leaves . . . and no more olives. There was only one good thing left: plenty of firewood.

Then Saleem noticed Nada standing in the doorway of her kitchen. Slowly she came over to the broken wall.

"They always told me about this tree," she said quietly. "I wondered if I would ever see it. It was so old and beautiful, they said, and gave such good olives. I thought this tree was really like my home, my parents' and grandparents' home that they nearly lost. And now it's gone."

Saleem wanted to say that it was the Besharas' own fault that they'd nearly lost their home; they hadn't had to leave. But what good would that do? Instead he looked once more around the wood-strewn yard, then turned back to Nada.

"Anyway," he said, "you'll be warm this winter." He picked up a couple of large chunks of wood, stepped over the broken wall, and laid the wood in Nada's yard.

Saleem made several more trips, carrying wood to Nada's yard. Then he stopped short in surprise.

Nada was busy doing the very same thing in Saleem's yard.

All morning the two worked in silence, clearing the olive wood and stacking it neatly against each other's houses.

When at last Saleem went in for lunch, he found on the wood chair by his door a little heap of olives, carefully salvaged from among the splinters and withering leaves.

Andy
–and–
Wong Pao

by Ann Poland

"Well, Ella has quit and that's that," Andy's mother said. "I don't know who I will get to stay with you after school from now on."

"I'm big enough to stay alone, Mother. And I'm not afraid."

"I know you are not afraid. But I don't want you staying alone."

Andy Watkins and his mother lived together in an apartment building, and Mrs. Watkins had to work to earn their living. They were happy together, but sometimes things were hard, and Andy knew his mother got discouraged. They left home at the same time in the morning. Andy ate lunch at the cafeteria at school, but he got out at three-thirty and his mother didn't get home until five-thirty.

"Let's not worry about it tonight," Andy's mother said. "It's Friday evening, and we have the whole weekend to work things out. Why don't we go down the block to Wong Pao's restaurant and have a chop-suey supper? That always makes us feel better."

"Oh, boy, it sure does!" Andy loved to eat at The Jade Lantern. Wong Pao was a kind, gentle man who liked people and seemed to have all sorts of knowledge in his head.

As Andy and his mother went into the restaurant, Wong Pao greeted them at the door, as he did all his customers. "Good evening, my friends, Mrs. Watkins and young Andy. Would you like a table by the window tonight? I trust you are both well and happy."

"We are well, thank you," Mrs. Watkins said as they sat down. "But I guess we are not so happy. In fact, we have a problem."

"My sitter has quit," Andy explained. "She got a better job that pays her more money. So now we have nobody, and Mother does not want me to be alone after school."

"She is right. A boy of your age should not be home alone."

"But I wouldn't get into any trouble."

"Not trouble, no. But a boy needs someone— someone to look to when he has a need." Then a thoughtful look came over Mr. Pao's face. He turned to Mrs. Watkins. "Why couldn't Andy stay here with me in the restaurant until you come from your job?"

Andy and Mrs. Watkins looked at each other. "Oh, we wouldn't want to trouble you," Mrs. Watkins said.

"It would be no trouble. It would be a pleasure to have Andy here. If you would feel better, he could do chores around the kitchen."

"Sure, I could do that," Andy said. He thought it would be really fine, staying with Wong Pao.

"All right, then," Andy's mother said. So on Monday, Andy began going to The Jade Lantern after school.

Andy was happy, and for many days everything went well with him. But one day Andy went into the restaurant's kitchen to slice vegetables. He worked slowly and with very little spirit.

"Something troubles you?" asked Wong Pao.

"Yes," Andy sighed. "For one thing, my mother is tired and has not felt like cleaning up the apartment. It's a real mess and it bothers her. Then I have twelve math problems to do, and they are hard ones. I have to have them done by tomorrow. And on top of that, I fell today playing ball and tore a hole in the knee of my last pair of jeans. I know my mother does not have enough money just now to buy another pair."

"The world sits on your shoulders," Wong Pao said thoughtfully.

"That's just what it feels like."

"Well, perhaps tomorrow it will feel as if the world is all under your feet."

"What do you mean?"

"Come, look at this bowl on the shelf."

Wong Pao took down a bowl with an emblem painted on it. He pointed to it and said, "See the two sides of the circle divided by the curved line? These tell us the two sides of life—*yin*, which means darkness, and *yang*, which means light. The two sides alternate. One day the sun shines on you and another day the sun won't shine. The person who can understand the two sides is happy and wise. For centuries the Chinese have believed that the secret of a happy life is to try to keep a harmony, or balance, between the two sides."

Andy looked at the symbol and listened to what Wong Pao was saying. "That's interesting," he said. But he did not really understand. He said, "It's hard to see why there has to be darkness at all."

Wong Pao nodded. "We do not like to see the darkness, but people have learned that even though we do not understand, it is the way that things are. Perhaps we appreciate the light more after the darkness."

Andy was thoughtful and silent for a while. Then he had another question. "But when things are in darkness, how do they get changed back into light again?"

"There is no magic way. Each seems to have its own time of coming and staying and then going again. But each day we must do what we can in our own lives to keep the harmony and not be disturbed by the things that go wrong. But now I must get back to my customers. If you like, you may keep the bowl."

"Thank you." Andy then went back to slicing vegetables, but he kept looking at the bowl and thinking about what Wong Pao had said.

That evening when Andy and his mother were back in the apartment and he was still thinking of Wong Pao's words, he showed his mother the bowl with the emblem on it. She smiled and listened to what he had to say. But Andy could see the tired look in her eyes. He had an idea.

"Mother," he said, "why don't you go take a nap? I am going to make a surprise for you." He took her arm gently and led her to her bedroom. When the door was shut, he went back to the kitchen.

First he looked in the refrigerator. There was left-over meat loaf, some cold boiled potatoes, and a package of frozen corn. He wrapped the meat loaf in foil and put it in the oven to warm up. Then he chopped up the potatoes in the skillet to brown and put the corn in a pan with butter to heat. In the crisper drawer he found lettuce for a salad.

Then he gathered up the clothing he had left thrown around his room, hung up all the clean things, and put the dirty ones in the hamper. He straightened up all the magazines and papers. He got a dustcloth and worked it quickly over the furniture. Finally he got out the vacuum, but decided to wait to run it until his mother woke up. But things looked a lot better, and he felt better.

While his mother still slept, Andy went to his desk in the dining room and sat down to work on the math problems. He put his bowl on the desk so he could look at it now and then. As he sat down, the rip in his jeans ripped a little farther. Maybe his mother would have one of those iron-on patches that would make them do for a while longer. The math problems were hard, but he did the best he could. He was surprised to find that he was more than half-finished when he heard his mother coming in from the bedroom.

"My, something smells good!" she said. Then she looked around. "Why, Andy, you've fixed supper and cleaned the apartment."

Andy smiled and said, "All but running the vacuum. I didn't want to wake you. But after supper, I'll finish my math, and take care of the vacuuming, and then I'll do the dishes." She hugged him, and he was glad to see his mother look rested and pleased.

As they went in to eat their supper, Andy looked at his bowl and said a silent "thank you." The bowl and its story would not solve all his problems, but it would help. He decided he would always keep it near him with his other treasures.

A Rupee Goes a
Long Way

By Ruskin Bond

Ranji had a one-rupee coin. He'd had it since morning, and now it was afternoon—and that was far too long to keep a rupee. It was time he spent the money, or some of it, or most of it.

Ranji had made a list in his head of all the things he wanted to buy and all the things he wanted to eat. But he knew that with only one rupee in his pocket the list wouldn't get much shorter. His tummy, he decided, should be given first choice. So he made his way to the Jumna Sweet Shop, tossed the coin on the counter, and asked for a rupee's worth of *jalebis*—those spangled, golden sweets made of flour and sugar that are so popular in India.

The shopkeeper picked up the coin, looked at it carefully, and set it back on the counter. "That coin's no good," he said.

"Are you sure?" Ranji asked.

"Look," said the shopkeeper, holding up the coin. "It's got England's King George on one side. These coins went out of use long ago. If it was one of the older ones—like Queen Victoria's, made of silver—it would be worth something for the silver, much more than a rupee. But this isn't a silver rupee. So, you see, it isn't old enough to be valuable, and it isn't new enough to buy anything."

Ranji looked from the coin to the shopkeeper to the chains of hot *jalebis* sizzling in a pan. He shrugged, took the coin back, and turned onto the road. There was no one to blame for the coin.

Ranji wandered through the bazaar. He gazed after the passing balloon man, whose long pole was hung with balloons of many colors. They were only twenty paise each—he could have had five for a rupee—but he didn't have any more change.

He was watching some boys playing marbles and wondering whether he should join them, when he heard a familiar voice behind him. "Where are you going, Ranji?"

It was Mohinder Singh, Ranji's friend. Mohinder's turban was too big for him and was almost falling over his eyes. In one hand he held a homemade fishing rod, complete with hook and line.

"I'm not going anywhere," said Ranji. "Where are you going?"

"I'm not going, I've *been*," Mohinder said. "I was fishing in the canal all morning."

Ranji stared at the fishing rod. "Will you lend it to me?" he asked.

"You'll only lose it or break it," Mohinder said. "But I don't mind selling it to you. Two rupees. Is that too much?"

"I've got one rupee," said Ranji, showing his coin. "But it's an old one. The sweet-seller would not take it."

"Please let me see it," said Mohinder.

He took the coin and looked it over as though he knew all about coins. "Hmmm . . . I don't suppose it's worth much, but my uncle collects old coins. Give it to me and I'll give you the rod."

"All right," said Ranji, only too happy to make the exchange. He took the fishing rod, waved good-bye to Mohinder, and set off. Soon he was on the main road leading out of town.

After some time a truck came along. It was on its way to the quarries near the riverbed, where it would be loaded with limestone. Ranji knew the driver, and waved and shouted to him until he stopped.

"Will you take me to the river?" Ranji asked. "I'm going fishing."

There was already someone sitting up front with the driver. "Climb up in the back," he said. "And don't lean over the side."

Ranji climbed into the back of the open truck. Soon he was watching the road slide away from him. They quickly passed bullock carts, cyclists, and a long line of camels. Motorists honked their horns as dust from the truck whirled up in front of them.

Soon the truck stopped near the riverbed. Ranji got down, thanked the driver, and began walking along the bank. It was the dry season, and the river was just a shallow, muddy stream. Ranji walked up and down without finding water deep enough for the smallest of fish.

"No wonder Mohinder let me have his rod," he muttered. And with a shrug he turned back toward town.

It was a long, hot walk back to the bazaar. Ranji walked slowly along the dusty road, swiping at bushes with his fishing rod. There were ripe mangoes on the trees, and Ranji tried to get at a few of them with the tip of the rod, but they were well out of reach. The sight of all those mangoes made his mouth water, and he thought again of the *jalebis* that he hadn't been able to buy.

He had reached a few scattered houses when he saw a barefoot boy playing a flute. In the stillness of the hot afternoon the cheap flute made a cheerful sound.

Ranji stopped walking. The boy stopped playing. They stood there, sizing each other up. The boy had his eye on Ranji's fishing rod; Ranji had his eye on the flute.

"Been fishing?" asked the flute player.

"Yes," said Ranji.

"Did you catch anything?"

"No," said Ranji. "I didn't stay very long."

"Did you see any fish?"

"The water was very muddy."

There was a long silence. Then Ranji said, "It's a good rod."

"This is a good flute," said the boy.

Ranji took the flute and examined it. He put it to his lips and blew hard. There was a shrill, squeaky noise, and a startled magpie flew out of a mango tree.

"Not bad," said Ranji.

The boy had taken the rod from Ranji and was looking it over. "Not bad," he said.

Ranji hesitated no longer. "Let's exchange."

A trade was made, and the barefoot boy rested the fishing rod on his shoulder and went on his way, leaving Ranji with the flute.

Ranji began playing the flute, running up and down the scale. The notes sounded lovely to him, but they startled people who were passing on the road.

After a while Ranji felt thirsty and drank water from a roadside tap. When he came to the clock tower, where the bazaar began, he sat on the low wall and blew vigorously on the flute. Several children gathered around, thinking he might be a snake charmer. When no snake appeared, they went away.

"I can play better than that," said a boy who was carrying several empty milk cans.

"Let's see," Ranji said.

The boy took the flute and put it to his lips and played a lovely little tune.

"You can have it for a rupee," said Ranji.

"I don't have any money to spare," said the boy. "What I get for my milk I have to take home. But you can have this necklace."

He showed Ranji a pretty necklace of brightly colored stones.

"I'm not a girl," said Ranji.

"I didn't say you had to wear it. You can give it to your sister."

"I don't have a sister."

"Then you can give it to your mother," said the boy. "Or your grandmother. The stones are very precious. They were found in the mountains near Tibet."

Ranji was tempted. He knew the stones had little value, but they were pretty. And he was tired of the flute.

They made the exchange, and the boy went off playing the flute. Ranji was about to thrust the necklace into his pocket when he noticed a girl staring at him. Her name was Koki and she lived close to his house.

"Hello, Koki," he said, feeling rather silly with the necklace still in his hands.

"What's that you've got, Ranji?"

"A necklace. It's pretty, isn't it? Would you like to have it?"

"Oh, thank you," said Koki, clapping her hands with pleasure.

"One rupee," said Ranji.

"Oh," said Koki.

She made a face, but Ranji was looking the other way and humming. Koki kept staring at the necklace. Slowly she opened a little purse, took out a shining new rupee, and held it out to Ranji.

Ranji handed her the necklace. The coin felt hot in his hand. It wasn't going to stay there for long. Ranji's stomach was rumbling. He ran across the street to the Jumna Sweet Shop and tossed the coin on the counter.

"*Jalebis* for a rupee," he said.

The sweet-seller picked up the coin, studied it carefully, then gave Ranji a toothy smile and said, "Always at your service, sir." He filled a paper bag with hot *jalebis* and handed them over.

When Ranji reached the clock tower, he found Koki waiting.

"Oh, I'm so hungry," she said, giving him a shy smile.

So they sat side by side on the low wall, and Koki helped Ranji finish the *jalebis*.

Maria and Masha

By Laurie Samsel Olson

One day Maria's teacher, Miss Jones, came to class excited. "Children," she said, "we are very lucky to be chosen for a special project. We are going to write letters to children in Russia and they are going to write back to us."

Jimmy, the boy who sat next to Maria, raised his hand. "But how can we do that?" he asked. "We don't speak the same language."

"Children in Russia begin to learn another language, usually English, by the time they are in their third year of school," Miss Jones answered. "Of course, it takes a long time to learn a new language well. So, for this project, a person in Russia who speaks English well will translate your letters into Russian so the Russian students can read them. Someone here who knows the Russian language will translate the letters from the Russian students into English so you can read them."

Maria sat quietly. She thought the project sounded fine. But she didn't know what she should write to a child in Russia. Russia was thousands of miles away, clear across the ocean. The people were sure to be very different. Maria guessed that a little girl in Russia probably didn't like any of the same things she did. Still, when Miss Jones said to take out pencil and paper, Maria began to write.

Dear Friend,

My name is Maria. I am ten years old. In my fifth grade class I study math, reading, spelling, health, English, science, and history. I like reading best.

I have one brother whose name is Adam. He is eight years old and we fight a lot, but I like him anyway.

For fun I like to jump rope and draw pictures. I go to Girl Scouts every Thursday.

We like to make things and visit a special
home for old people. What do you like to do?
> *Love,*
> *Maria*

About two weeks after the class wrote their letters, a stack of mail arrived from Russia. There was a letter for everyone. Maria carefully unfolded hers. There was more than one sheet. One page had Russian words spelled with many letters Maria had never seen. Another had English words.

Dear Maria,

At first I was not sure this project would be fun. I thought you probably didn't like any of the same things I do. But your letter was nice, and I found out we are very much alike.

I am also ten years old. Our schools are a little different from yours, so I am only in my fourth year of classes. Some of the things I study are math, science, Russian, and English.

Like you, I like to read and I have a brother, Peter. He likes to tease me.

We don't have Girl Scouts in Russia but we do have something like it. It is called

Young Pioneers. We work on many projects to help the community. In the summer we go to camp.

One of the best things about your letter was your name. It is the same as mine—Maria! My nickname is Masha. I hope we can write to each other again.

Love,
Masha

Maria smiled. She was glad to have a new friend in a country so far away. She knew Masha felt that way, too, when she looked at the last page of her letter.

It was a drawing of two little girls. One was standing in a yellow circle marked "Russia" and the other was on a green circle marked "America." Over the blue ocean between them, the girls—one called Maria and the other called Masha—were holding hands.

An Arctic Welcome

By Marie Ward

The first snow of winter had come in the night.

"A good sign," Matthew's mother said as she dipped water from a bucket into the teakettle. "See how the snow sparkles on the schoolhouse. It is a welcome to the new teacher."

Matthew stretched to see over the windowsill and looked for a sign of an airplane in the pale morning sky. He listened for the hum of the engine that would bring the new teacher, but there was only the silence of the Arctic.

His mother set the kettle on the round barrel stove. She placed jars of blueberry jam in a shallow basket she had woven of bay grass. It was a gift for the teacher.

"I have nothing to give," Matthew said sadly.

"Didn't you help pick the berries for the jam?" his mother asked.

"But she will never know which blueberries I picked. They are all squashed together. Samuel carved an ivory seal for her." He remembered the day his cousin had found the walrus tusk lying on the beach, poking up in the sand like driftwood. It was so big that the boys knew many animals hid within it, waiting to be carved. Samuel was lucky.

All day, as Matthew played outdoors, he tried to think of something special he could give the new teacher. There had been talk all summer about how there might not be a teacher for the dark winter days ahead. None had been found to replace Mrs. Norman, who had gone to a city far away. Then, on the August day when the summer sun slipped behind the ocean and the sky darkened for the first time since spring, a letter came to the chief. The village would have a teacher.

Matthew kicked an ice-covered stone. It broke loose from the road gravel and rolled away into the thin snow dusting the tundra. He reached for the rock. Turning it this way and that, he tried to see the face of a seal in it or maybe a bear. But all he saw was a rock.

What he really wanted to find was something beautiful, something really special. He shut his eyes tightly and thought.

When Matthew opened his eyes he was surprised to see something twinkling from an umiak on the beach. Among the fish netting draped over the boat's bow were delicate ice crystals, clear and glistening in the sun. The tiny threads of icy lace reminded Matthew of jewelry that a queen might wear.

He smiled. He knew he had found something the teacher would like.

It was late afternoon when an airplane hummed over the choppy sea and skidded along the snow-covered runway on skis.

The pilot handed down the mail, and two passengers got off. There was the public health nurse, who had come for her regular visit, and a bearded man with black skin. The man wore a big, billowing yellow parka.

But nowhere did Matthew see the new teacher.

Matthew was standing by Lucy and Mary, who were giggling together. They were older than he was and always had many secrets.

"I don't see the teacher," Matthew said to them.

"Then open your eyes," Lucy said. "He's right over there." The girls giggled again, covering their mouths so that an elder wouldn't scold them for being impolite.

"It sure will seem strange," Matthew said.

People were welcoming the man with handshakes as they ushered him into the *cashim*, the meetinghouse. The potlach celebration was beginning. There would be food, dances in the old way, and, later in the night, fiddle and guitar music for dancing in the modern way. It would be a big celebration to honor the teacher.

Everyone was happy, except Matthew. He had been sure that a woman teacher would like the glistening ice crystals, but a man made him unsure. That was why he put off walking up to the teacher for so long. The food was nearly gone, and still he hesitated. If Samuel had not come along at that moment, Matthew would have lost his nerve.

"Mr. Hunter liked my carving," Samuel said.

It was the way Samuel swaggered that gave Matthew the final push. He walked right up to Mr. Hunter and stared into his face.

"I have something special I would like you to see," Matthew said. "It's outside."

"A little fresh air sounds good to me," Mr. Hunter said and gave Matthew a big, warm smile. He pulled on his odd yellow parka and mittens.

The moment they stepped into the clear, cold night, Matthew realized his mistake. In the darkness there would be no dazzling ice crystals to show. He flushed with embarrassment.

But Matthew was surprised to hear Mr. Hunter's voice. "This is fantastic! I have never seen anything so spectacular."

"What?" Matthew stammered. Then he realized Mr. Hunter was looking up at a beautiful display of northern lights.

"Look at those colors. Do you get the aurora this bright and colorful often?"

"Yes, often, especially in the fall and spring," Matthew said proudly.

"Well, thank you, Matthew, for showing me what has to be one of the greatest shows on earth. This is teriffic!" Mr. Hunter put his hand on Matthew's shoulder, and they watched until the dancing lights faded and a fiddle could be heard. Together they walked back to the *cashim*.

Shing Lee
and the
Sampan

By Bernadine Beatie

Shing Lee waited impatiently while Mrs. Chung folded his clothes and tied them into a neat bundle. Shing Lee's grandfather had sent him ashore to stay with Hai Chung and his wife during the school term. But now school was out and Shing Lee could hardly wait to get to the harbor. He smiled. Grandfather would be waiting there in his sampan. Ah, he would have a fine summer fishing with his grandfather!

Mrs. Chung frowned. "You are a foolish boy," she said. "You should tell your grandfather of the fine job Yu Tang offered you. Guiding tourists about the streets of Hong Kong would be much easier and safer than fishing in that leaky old sampan with your grandfather."

Shing Lee smiled. "You would not have me desert my grandfather? Fishing is the only life he knows. He would be very sad away from the sea."

"Your grandfather should find work ashore. Someday he will realize that a small sailing craft like his cannot compete with the motorized junks and sampans of the younger fishermen."

"My grandfather and I have talked of this," Shing Lee said. "He may decide that we too must have a motor for our boat."

"I still think you should work for Yu Tang. With your knowledge of English, he would find many tourists for you to guide. Besides, I shall worry about you, Shing Lee." There was sadness on the face of Mrs. Chung.

"Do not worry, Honorable One," Shing Lee said softly. "My grandfather is a good sailor. I shall come to see you often."

After the first excitement and happiness of being back on the sampan with his grandfather faded, Shing Lee was surprised and just a bit frightened. Nothing was as he remembered it. Grandfather looked old and tired. The sampan seemed small and shabby.

"Have the catches been good, Grandfather?" Shing Lee asked.

"Not too good," Grandfather said. Then he smiled. "But now that I have you to help with the nets, the catch will be good once more."

"And the motor, Grandfather? Have you thought of that?"

"It is sad to think that soon there will be no junks and sampans running before the breeze, their bright sails fluttering like the wings of giant birds," Grandfather sighed. "But you are right, my grandson, the old must always be replaced by the new. As soon as we have made enough money, we shall buy a motor."

Shing Lee's spirits rose. "That will be soon."

But as day followed day, the catch remained small, bringing in only a few coins each day. After Grandfather added to the small hoard he put aside for Shing Lee's schooling and bought rice and tea, there was nothing left.

A heaviness grew in Shing Lee's heart as he watched his grandfather. The sparkle was gone from his grandfather's eyes, and his hands trembled as he worked with the sail.

One afternoon Shing Lee and his grandfather took a gift of fish to Hai Chung and his wife.

When they were preparing to leave, Mrs. Chung spoke. "Yu Tang told me that he still has a place for you, guiding tourists, Shing Lee. He said that he could find work for you also, Honorable Old One, working in the garden of his wife's mother."

Shing Lee spoke quickly when he saw the surprise on his grandfather's face. "My grandfather is a fisherman," he said proudly. "I am honored to work with him."

As they walked back to the harbor, Grandfather spoke sadly. "Perhaps I am a foolish old man. Perhaps I should sell my boat. There would be enough money then for you to finish school. But I do not think I would be a good gardener."

Shing Lee's heart twisted. The joy would be gone from Grandfather's life if he left the sea.

"No, Grandfather," Shing Lee said. "We will think of something." He frowned. If only they had a motor. Then, when the fishing was bad, they could use their sampan as a water taxi and take passengers back and forth between the small islands. Shing Lee's eyes brightened. They did not have to have a motor to carry passengers. They would be slower than the motorized sampans, but they could charge less.

"It will do no harm to try," Grandfather said when Shing Lee told him of his plan.

Shing Lee and his grandfather worked late that night, scouring and polishing, and mending the sails of the sampan. And the next day, though Shing Lee cried out bravely, there were very few passengers. Shing Lee was discouraged, though he tried to hide it under a bright smile.

At the end of the third day Grandfather spoke. "Mrs. Chung is right, my grandson. You should be guiding tourists."

Shing Lee jumped to his feet, his face shining. "Tourists! That is the answer, Grandfather. Why did I not think of this before? I shall be a guide, Grandfather. I shall show tourists the sights from a sampan sailing around the harbor—a sampan with sails like the wings of a bird. You shall tell them stories of the old days, stories of pirates and fishing wars! Tonight I shall see my friend Yu Tang. I am sure that he will help."

That night Shing Lee went to the home of Yu Tang and outlined his plan. His heart was in his throat as he waited for Yu Tang's reply.

"Tourists like the old, romantic ways," Yu Tang said thoughtfully.

"My Grandfather and I will pay you commission on passengers you send us," Shing Lee said.

Yu Tang laughed. "We can arrange that easily enough. Wait at your sampan in the morning. Perhaps I shall have passengers for you."

The first day Yu Tang had three tourists who were eager for a sail on a real old-fashioned sampan. The second day there were six, and from then on the sampan was filled each day. Shing Lee watched the sparkle come back to his grandfather's eyes as he worked happily with the sail. Soon there was money enough for Shing Lee's schooling the next year.

"There is money enough for a motor, too," Grandfather said.

Shing Lee smiled. "But we do not need a motor now."

"Oh, yes, we do, though we shall use it only for fishing." Grandfather's dark eyes twinkled. "There is room in the world for the new as well as the old. You must remember that, my grandson, when you are old and have grandsons of your own." He smiled and his hand rested briefly on Shing Lee's shoulder. "My wish is that your grandsons will be as strong and brave as my own."

The Great Wax Dilemma

By Cindy Muscatel

On a frosty winter morning Cohen, the candlemaker, woke with a start when he heard a knocking sound. He jumped out of bed, pulling on his robe as he ran to answer the door.

"Joshua and Tami! Are you on your way to school?" he asked the children standing on the step.

"Yes, Mr. Candlemaker, but we stopped to remind you that Hanukkah is early this year," Tami said.

"You need to start the making candles now!" added Joshua.

"You are such good children to help me remember," Cohen said. "I'll begin today!"

After he had eaten his breakfast, he went to see Mr. Segal, owner of the Waxworks.

"Mr. Segal, it's time to start preparing for Hanukkah. I need one hundred pounds of wax!"

"That's twenty-five pounds more than last year!" Mr. Segal bellowed.

"Yes. We've got several new families. Everyone needs candles for the eight nights of Hanukkah."

"Well, I have only eighty-five pounds in stock," Mr. Segal snapped.

"But this means some families won't be able to celebrate Hanukkah," Cohen complained. "No potato pancakes, no parties, no presents, no playing dreidel, no songs . . ."

"Spare me your melodramatics, Candlemaker," Mr. Segal said.

"But what will we do?"

"You want wax, come to me. You want decisions, go see the mayor."

"Good idea!"

Cohen hurried over to the town hall.

"Calm down," the mayor said when he'd heard the story. "I'll call a meeting for five o'clock."

The candlemaker sat in the town hall, with Tami and Joshua beside him. It was so noisy the mayor had to pound on the table and shout, "Quiet, everybody!"

Finally he could begin. "We must solve this wax dilemma. Suggestions?"

"I say, 'First come, first served,'" one council member called out.

"The new people are the cause of the problem. They'll have to do without," said one woman.

"That's selfish," someone else answered. "If we all can't have Hanukkah candles, then none of us should have them!"

People shouted. The mayor pounded.

"Wait, listen!" Cohen yelled. He pushed Tami and Joshua forward. The townspeople stared at them. Each child was holding a candle stub.

"We could melt our old candles together to make new wax," Tami said.

"It's nice to share," added Joshua.

The mayor said, "A fantastic idea! I appoint you two children to organize the collection." He stopped. "It will work, Cohen, won't it?"

"I'll make it work!" Cohen answered.

Tami and Joshua organized the children, who collected barrels of candle stubs. The candlemaker melted the candles, added dyes, and poured the wax into molds. Soon his workshop was a rainbow of candles.

When Hanukkah came, the town held a celebration. There were potato pancakes and dreidel games, songs and dances. The rabbi told the story of the freedom-loving Maccabees.

"*Nes Gadol Haya Sham.* A great miracle happened here, too," he said. "Because of Cohen, Tami, and Joshua, who have *Tsedakah*, the spirit of sharing, we'll all share the glow of Hanukkah. They must light the candles!"

Tami, Joshua, and the candlemaker stood by the large menorah. The townspeople cheered, "Hip, Hip, Hooray!"

When Cohen crawled into bed that night, he glowed just as his beautiful candles had.

"I can't wait for next year," he said and fell asleep immediately.

The
Turban

By Dorothea C. Hill

Gambhir Singh's grandfather lay on a cot in the shade of the great salt cedar tree in the yard. Heat waves wriggled upward from the burning sand beyond the shade. It was hot, even for Imperial Valley, California—one of the hottest parts of the United States.

"I am going back to India to live," said Gambhir Singh's grandfather.

"No!" cried Gambhir, looking up from polishing a quartz crystal he had found on the desert. "You cannot leave us."

"Yes, I will go back to the Punjab where I was born." The old man's dark eyes gazed far away, almost as though he were seeing the dry, red plains of the Punjab in India.

A tightening came in Gambhir's throat.

"When I was born," Gambhir's grandfather continued, "I remember the maharajah came and kissed me on the forehead."

"But you could not remember the day that you were born."

"A great diamond shone like a star in the middle of his turban." Gambhir Singh's grandfather talked on as though Gambhir were not even there.

At the word *turban*, the tightness in Gambhir's throat choked him. After all these years in California, his grandfather still wore a turban. On Gambhir's recent birthday, his twelfth, his grandfather had given him a turban.

His grandfather had wound it expertly about Gambhir's head. "There. I want you to wear it. Besides being part of your heritage, it will protect you against sunstroke."

"But nobody here wears a turban!" Gambhir Singh exclaimed. He could have bitten his tongue off the minute he said it.

His grandfather had turned away, but not before Gambhir saw the hurt in his dark eyes.

To please Grandfather, Gambhir had worn the turban several times around home, but whenever he went off the ranch, he left it behind. One day his grandfather said, "You are ashamed of your Indian heritage."

Since that day, it was as though his grandfather had already gone back to India—he seemed so far far away.

Still, he could not wear a turban, Gambhir told himself. Not away from home. All of his friends would laugh at him.

But now he just had to do something.

Next morning Gambhir wound the turban around his head, drew the cloth tight, tucked in the ends—as his grandfather had shown him. "Bye-bye, Grandfather," he called cheerily as he walked off to school.

When he reached a clump of oleander beside the canal that carried water to their ranch, he laid down his books. Unwinding the turban, he folded it and hid it deep among the oleander leaves.

On the way home Gambhir searched out the turban and began to wind it around his head. He wished he had a mirror. However, feeling with his fingers, he did the best he could.

When he reached home, his grandfather was lying on the cot under the salt cedar. His eyes were closed, but when Gambhir said, "Hello, Grandfather," they opened.

At first the ends of Grandfather's white moustache lifted in a smile, but then they quickly drooped. "To be sure," he said, "it takes a lot of practice to put on a turban without a mirror."

In his room Gambhir looked in the mirror. The turban was a mess. It was rumpled; tails dangled; an oleander leaf stuck out crazily above his left ear.

That night Gambhir Singh lay awake for a long time. He had turned off the air-conditioning unit and opened the window. He could hear the frogs harrumphing in the canal and water running there.

Would his grandfather miss those things when he went back to India? Would Grandfather miss him, as he would miss his grandfather? Tears welled up in Gambhir's eyes.

The next morning Gambhir wound the turban around his head and went off to school.

When he returned that afternoon, his grandfather was not lying on the cot as usual—he was dusting off an old straw suitcase. When he saw Gambhir, he exclaimed, "What happened to you?"

"Fell down," said Gambhir. He walked past his grandfather and into his room.

When he looked in the mirror, he saw smudges on his face. His turban was also smudged and not very straight, but it was still on his head. It had been there all day. It was true—he had fallen, but not by accident. One of the boys who had been teasing him had stuck out his foot and tripped him.

Gambhir Singh put his turban into the washing machine and later hung it up to dry. Next morning he wound it neatly about his head. Then he trudged off to school.

When he returned that afternoon, his grandfather cried, "I suppose you fell down again?"

"Uh-huh."

Again Gambhir put his turban into the washer. Then he sat down and wrote a composition.

Again the following morning he wound the turban neatly about his head. This time Gambhir fastened the quartz crystal, which he had mounted on a jeweler's pin, to the front of the turban. When the crystal caught the light, it shone almost like a diamond.

That day when the teacher called on him, he got up and read his composition.

"The turban has been worn in India for thousands of years. It is a useful head covering. It keeps out heat as well as cold. Also, the turban is inexpensive. It is just one long piece of cloth. No sewing is necessary to make it. Once you have learned how to put on a turban, it is quite simple."

Gambhir took off his turban and showed how to put it on. "See, it is not difficult," he said proudly, "not for someone whose grandfather came from the Punjab in India."

When Gambhir Singh returned that day, his grandfather was putting clothes into the straw suitcase, which lay open on the cot under the salt cedar. "Grandfather," he said, "when you go back to India, I want you to send me something."

"And what do you want me to send you?" asked the old man, his eyes blinking in the dazzling light shining from the quartz crystal in Gambhir's turban.

"A dozen turbans."

"And what would you do with a dozen turbans?" asked his grandfather with surprise.

"Well, Grandfather, I want them for some of the boys at school. They think it is so hot here in the valley that it would be a good idea to wear turbans to protect them from the sun."

Gambhir Singh's grandfather was silent for a long time. At last, slowly, the ends of his white moustache lifted in a smile. "Would it be all right, Gambhir, if I just wrote to a shop in the Punjab and asked them to send us a dozen turbans?"

Gambhir's heart leaped for joy. However, he managed to keep a straight face when he said, "Well, Grandfather, I guess that would be all right."

Rodika

By Marianna Fülöp Crystal

Mayi lived in Transylvania, which means "across the woods." Transylvania was not a country or a state; it was more like a state of mind, which changed often. From time to time, this region was part of two different countries. Sometimes it was the southern part of Hungary, but just as often it was the northern tip of Romania.

In Transylvania, Romanians and Hungarians lived as neighbors, side by side. But they didn't always get along.

Mayi didn't know any of this, being a very young Hungarian. She lived in a house surrounded by a big garden and a tall fence. There were no children to play with, so she played alone. Oh, sometimes Grandmother played with her, by crocheting and watching, but mostly by telling her not to run and jump so much. Mother played with her by taking her for a walk in the park to visit the swans. Mayi had to wear white gloves, white socks, and pink ribbons in her hair, and she couldn't touch the grass.

Mayi's two funny uncles played with her, too. The one with thick glasses read stories, and the one who smelled of toast teased and made jokes.

But most of the time Mayi played her own secret games, making magic by twisting the fingers of both hands, one on top of the other, until they looked like pretzels. The magic kept her safe from the witch who lived in the dark, damp cellar, from the arms of the weeping willow that reached down to grab her, and from the wolves that lurked behind the trees, howling hungry *aoooooo's* that only she could hear.

One day, through a loose slat in the wooden fence, Mayi saw people move into the house next door. Soon a little girl appeared. She was somewhat bigger than Mayi, but still a person nearly her own size.

Mayi was very excited as she waved and called in Hungarian, "Hi, come here. Do you want to play?"

The girl said something that sounded like "*Gruschnikov skitankro.*" Then she pointed to herself and said "Rodika." Mayi raced home to get help. "There's a girl at the fence, but she talks funny. I can't understand her. Can she come over to play with me?" she asked.

"No," said Grandmother. "They're strangers."

"Romanian strangers," added Uncle Glasses. "They don't speak our language. How will you talk? It's rude to point."

Mayi ran back to the fence; she was not going to give up so easily on her first friend. But Rodika was gone.

The next morning, when everyone was out shopping except for Uncle Toast, Mayi and Rodika met again. They held each other's hands through the opening in the fence and sang songs, each in her own language, and knocked on a big snail's shell to make him come out. Then Rodika motioned for Mayi to squeeze through the fence.

The opening was small, but then so was Mayi, and she started to come across with Rodika pulling. All at once, she was stuck.

"Ouch, this hurts!" Mayi cried, but she could go neither forward nor backward. Tears were spilling freely when Rodika ran into her house and returned with her mother.

Together they managed to pull Mayi into their garden without major damage to her or the fence. Her scratches were cleaned, cookies were served, and the two girls played happily until they heard voices from the other garden getting louder and louder, calling, "Mayi, where are you?"

"Oh-oh," said Mayi.

"Uh-uh," said Rodika. They ran to the front, through the big gate and back around to Mayi's house, holding hands and skipping to show they were hardly scared.

When the family heard Mayi's story, there was a lot of laughter. "That was very nice of the lady, to get you out. Did you say thank you?" asked Mayi's Grandmother.

"They certainly sound like lovely people," said Uncle Glasses.

"Please don't go through the fence next time. Use the gate. And ask permission first," said Mother.

"They just didn't want a Hungarian stuck in their fence. That's why they removed you," said Uncle Toast. "Here, girls, have some lemonade."

"Can we get rid of the fence?" asked Mayi. "Rodika and I don't need it anymore."

And sure enough, they didn't.

Bombu's
Gift to the King

By Miriam Gilbert

Bombu was a little boy who lived behind a jungle, behind a river, behind a desert. He lived so far away from other people that he knew only the people of his tribe. He lived so far away from animals that he knew only the peaceful animals that lived on the land that belonged to his tribe.

One day high above the jungle, across the river, and up over the desert came a smoke signal.

"What is that?" Bombu asked his mother.

"All the tribes have a new king," said his mother.

Just then came the booming sounds of a drum.

"What is that?" Bombu asked his father.

"All the tribes are gathering together to celebrate the crowning of the king," said his father.

"Are we going?" Bombu asked excitedly.

"No," said his mother. "It is a long journey."

"Besides," added his father, "we have nothing to take to the king as a gift."

"We could take him some of mother's bread," Bombu said hopefully. "It is the best bread in the world, fit for a king."

His father shook his head. "No, a king must be given something very special, like gold or silver or precious jewels."

"We could give him some of your dried rattlesnake skin to make a belt," Bombu said. "It would make the most beautiful belt in the world, fit for a king."

"No," said his father, "we need something better, something wonderful and rare."

Bombu watched the smoke signals. Bombu listened to the booming drums.

"Mother, do you love me?" Bombu asked her suddenly.

Bombu's mother looked at him in surprise. "Of course I love you. To me you are more precious than all the jewels in the world."

"Father, do you love me?" Bombu asked.

Bombu's father smiled. "Little one, you are a tease. Of course I love you. To me you are more precious than all the fine tiger skins in the world."

"Then I am going to see the king crowned," Bombu said. "Maybe the king will think I am precious, too."

Bombu's mother and father looked at each other. Then Bombu's mother went into their hut and came out with a piece of bread, carefully wrapped in a large palm leaf. "This is for the king from Bombu's mother," she said.

Bombu's father went into their hut and came out with a long strip of dried rattlesnake skin. "This is for the king from Bombu's father," he said.

"I do not have a present now," Bombu said, "but I will think of something on my journey."

Bombu's mother kissed him. "Keep safe and well," she said.

Bombu started across the desert. He had not gone many miles, when he grew tired. In the shadow of a rock, a camel was resting.

"May I share the shade with you?" he asked.

The camel blinked his long eyelashes.

"I'm going to see the king crowned," Bombu said. "Why don't you come along? It will be nice to have a friend with me."

When Bombu started off, the camel followed behind him.

After many miles, Bombu came to a river. He stopped to wash his hands and face. As he was splashing, Bombu saw a crocodile in the water.

"I'm going to see the king crowned," Bombu said.

The crocodile yawned, showing his big teeth.

"Why don't you come with me?" Bombu said. "You must be my friend. You did not bite me."

When Bombu started off, the crocodile had fallen in line behind the camel.

After many miles, Bombu came to the jungle. The smoke signals were big and black now. The drums were beating so loudly that the ground was shaking. Bombu started to hurry. But there, curled up in the middle of the road, was a huge snake.

"I'm going to see the king crowned," Bombu said. "It should be very exciting. Why don't you come with me?"

The snake uncurled and let Bombu pass. Then he fell in line behind the crocodile.

After many more miles, Bombu came to a big clearing. Here he saw a large crowd of people. He didn't know where to go. The animals stayed behind at the edge of the clearing. Bombu looked around. Far over to one side was a man, all by himself, sitting in a chair.

Bombu approached timidly. "Please, sir," he said, "could you tell me where the king is?"

"Why do you wish to see the king?" the man said. "No one can approach the king who does not bring a gift of gold or silver or something rare." The man sounded angry. "What do you have for the king?"

"I have nothing," Bombu said. "My mother sent a piece of her bread for the king. My father sent a long strip of his rattlesnake skin for a belt." Bombu hung his head. "But I have nothing. I was too busy making some new friends. They are hungry. Do you think I could get some food for a camel, a crocodile, and a snake?"

"That is impossible!" the man thundered. "Everyone knows the camel is afraid of the crocodile, and the snake would bite the camel."

"How can they be afraid of each other?" Bombu said. "They all wanted to be friends so they could see the king crowned."

"Let me see," the man demanded.

Bombu waved to the animals. As the camel came forward, followed by the crocodile and the snake, a hush fell over the crowd.

"O King," said a tall man, stepping forth with a gold crown on a silver platter, "this is the sign we have been waiting for."

Bombu stared at the man in the chair, and his knees began to tremble. "Are you the king?" he asked fearfully.

The man put his hand gently on Bombu's shoulder. "Yes, I am, little one. And you have brought me the best present of all. If animals of all kinds can live together as friends, then I can help people of all kinds to live together as friends. I did not want to be crowned king until I felt there was some hope that the different tribes throughout our country could live together happily. Now I believe there is a chance."

The king took Bombu by the hand. "Come," he said, "I want you to stand at my side while I am crowned."

Mystery
of the
Red Duck

By Bonnie Highsmith Taylor

In the Norwegian village of Grimstad lived a little girl named Kari who had a white pet duck named Greta. Kari loved Greta more than anything in the world.

Every morning Kari would rush to the wooden-box house on the back porch and say to Greta, "*God Morgen*" (Good morning.)

Greta would flap her wings and answer, "Quack, quack!"

Always, when Kari looked in Greta's nest she would find a fresh egg for her breakfast.

"*Takk* (thank you), Greta," she would say.

Then she would fill Greta's trough with cracked corn and her tin dish with cool, sweet water from the well.

How Kari loved her duck. And how proud she felt when she walked along the road with Greta quacking at her heels.

"What a pretty duck!" Fru Olsen, who made jellies and pastries for the village market, would exclaim. What fine cakes her eggs would make."

Kari would only nod and walk on.

"*God morgen*, Kari," Herr Rolig, the actor-clown who performed in the village theater, would greet her. "What a fine act I would have if I owned such a duck. The tricks I could teach her!"

Kari would smile and hurry on her way.

When she passed the big farm at the edge of town, Herr Bonde would come running from the barn. "Ah, Kari, how I envy you! If I had such a duck, what fine ducklings I could raise for market. Please sell her to me."

"Never!" Kari would cry. "Not for all the money in the land."

And once when Kari and Greta strayed too close to the ramshackle cottage where Froken

Haksä lived, the old woman sprang out from the bushes. "Someday I shall have that duck," she cackled. "Mark my words. What magic her feet and bill would add to my brew."

Kari snatched up her pet and raced all the way to her house.

Never would Kari part with her beautiful duck.

But one morning, when Kari went to the wooden-box house on the porch, she found not a snowy white duck, but a bright red duck.

Her eyes grew wide with wonder. "Greta!" she cried. "What has happened to you?"

Greta quacked sadly and hung her head.

Kari could think of no reason for the sudden change in her pet. Yesterday she was white as a spring cloud; today she was bright red.

An idea popped into her head. "Froken Haksä has done this!" she shouted. "She has cast a magic spell!"

With Greta close behind, Kari ran boldly through the woods into the swampland. She banged furiously on the door of the shack. "Open the door!" she shouted in anger. "Open the door at once!"

Slowly the rusty hinges creaked open and the terrible old woman's face appeared.

"What have you done to Greta?" Kari demanded.

Froken Haksä glanced down at the girl's pet. "Eeek!" she shrieked. "A red duck!" She slammed the door in Kari's face. "Take it away! Take it away!"

Puzzled, Kari trudged on to the farm of Herr Bonde. "Please, sir," she said, "can you tell me what has happened to my duck?"

The farmer scratched his head. "This is a great mystery, indeed. Never have I heard of such a thing. I cannot explain it."

Kari traveled sadly on till she came to the house of Herr Rolig. But the clown was no help. "She has stayed too long in the sun," he laughed. "It is only sunburn."

Perhaps Fru Olsen will know, Kari thought, hurrying to see her.

"Oh, Fru Olsen," Kari blurted when she answered the door, "can you help me solve my mystery?"

"Be off with you, girl," Fru Olsen said impatiently. "I have no time for games. Besides, I have a mystery of my own."

"Mystery?" the bewildered girl asked.

"Feathers in my berry juice, that's what mystery," Fru Olsen yelled angrily. "All day yesterday my children and I worked to pick berries to make jelly for the market. And this morning, what do I find? Feathers in my berry juice. Everyone knows berries do not have feathers!"

Kari swallowed hard and looked about for Greta. But Greta was nowhere to be seen.

Suddenly a loud splashing sound came from the shed beside the cottage.

Kari and Fru Olsen arrived on the scene at the same time. There, splashing and dipping in a large wooden tub of berry juice, was Greta.

Kari was speechless. She could feel her heart pounding in her chest. What would Fru Olsen do to her beloved pet?

But—Fru Olsen was laughing! She was laughing so hard the tears were streaming down her cheeks.

"But—but—" Kari stammered. "You are not angry? You will not harm my pet?"

"Not if you promise to pick me some more berries," Fru Olsen answered. "And don't worry about Greta. In a few weeks she will be as white as ever."

"It's good to have the mystery solved," Kari smiled. "Both of them."

BRAVO,

THE GARLIC-BREATHING DONKEY

By Ethel H. Naugle

The donkey braying outside woke Vasos, and he jumped out of bed. Vasos looked at his rock collection as he pulled on patched pants and a shirt. Perhaps today Papa would not need him to go to town.

But Papa sat at the kitchen table, braiding the garlic into ropes. "Good morning, Vasos." Papa smiled. "Today you and Bravo may sell the garlic by yourselves. You are a big boy." Papa's thick fingers flew along the fat bulbs.

Vasos hated riding the small donkey and yelling "*skordho!*" all day while the customers pinched the garlic and counted out *drachmas*. He wanted to go to the harbor and watch the boats, or search the hills for rocks to add to his collection.

But Vasos gathered the strands of garlic and slung them over his shoulders. He nodded to his father and hurried out the door.

"Good luck!" Papa called after him. "Mama will make you a squid stew for supper."

Bravo, the family's chocolate-colored donkey, lifted his head over the fence and brayed.

"Shhh. You will wake up the neighborhood," said Vasos. He broke off a clove of garlic and held it out to Bravo. The donkey nibbled the garlic and rubbed his head against Vasos's shoulder.

Vasos and Bravo headed down the rocky path. The Greek island of Thira was bathed in the sun's rosy light. Vasos looked down toward the sea. A bright orange rock on the hill below caught his eye. He hung the ropes of garlic on the fence and carefully climbed down the hill.

The hillside was full of colorful rocks, and Vasos gathered several. Then he sat and watched a white boat drop anchor in the harbor.

Bravo's voice shattered the stillness, and Vasos ran back up the hill. He reached for the garlic, but it was not there. Vasos looked around. Crushed bulbs of garlic lay scattered along the fence.

"Bravo. You chewed it up! Now what will we have to sell?"

Vasos took the rocks out of his pocket and flung them over the fence. He sat down with his head in his hands.

Then he jumped up. "Tourists on the boats pay many *drachmas* to ride donkeys up from the harbor. Come, Bravo." He led the donkey past the whitewashed houses, down the rocky path, and past the brilliant blue dome of the church. Soon they reached the stone steps that led down to the harbor.

"One hundred *drachmas*?" asked a woman, counting the coins into Vasos's hand. Vasos helped her into the saddle. "Phew," the woman said. "What is that smell?"

Vasos led Bravo slowly up the steps. At every turn Bravo stopped, and Vasos had to coax him to move. Vasos counted the steps. They climbed up 587 steps and they climbed down 587 steps. All day, as the sun grew hotter, Vasos and Bravo trudged up and down the steps while the tourists rode on Bravo's back.

When the sun was low in the sky, Bravo opened his mouth wide and wheezed. A big girl in a red dress sat in the saddle and laughed. She kicked Bravo in the ribs. "Go, you smelly old slowpoke. Go." And she kicked Bravo hard with both heels.

Vasos turned and glared at the girl. He wiped the sweat out of his eyes. "Don't kick the one who is good enough to carry you!" he shouted. He stroked Bravo's ear. "Come," he whispered. Bravo slowly climbed up the next step.

When they reached the top Vasos helped the girl down and pocketed her coins. Then he and Bravo headed toward home.

In the kitchen, Vasos emptied his heavy pockets onto the table.

"So may *drachmas*," Papa said with alarm. "Did you cheat my customers?"

Vasos shook his head. For an instant, he thought about telling a lie. "I wanted a piece of orange pumice," he said. "While I was gone, Bravo chewed up the garlic. But we went down to the harbor, and all day we ferried the tourists up the steps. Of course, they complained about Bravo's smell."

Papa frowned, and Vasos's knees trembled.

"I am sorry, Papa."

"So." Papa drummed on the table with his thick fingers.

"Tomorrow, Papa, I will sell all of the garlic."

"Did you feed Bravo some oats?"

"Oh, yes. And I filled the trough with plenty of fresh water, too."

Papa smiled. He patted Vasos on the head. He picked up the *drachmas* and let them slide through his fingers. Mama came from the stove with a bowl of stew.

"This is for my Vasoplaki," she said as she set the steaming bowl on the table. She pulled a roll of peppermint drops from her pocket. "And these are for Bravo."

She wrinkled her nose, and they all laughed.

Una Piñata Para Los Pobres

By Virginia Kroll

One magic morning Mama said, "Pedro, after school you may go to the market and pick out all the treats."

Pedro's breath caught.

"And," Papa added, "you may choose the piñata yourself."

Pedro whooped. He hugged Mama quickly and gripped Papa's shoulders. Then he stuffed his sleeves inside his jacket and started off the school.

Ever since Pedro could remember, his family had had *posadas*—parties with songs, games, food, and especially, a piñata to break—before Christmastime. It was a tradition that the family had brought from Mexico.

The *posadas* always started out the same way. Friends and neighbors pretended to be the weary Christmas travelers, begging for lodging as they did so long ago. When they were finally let in, the fiesta would begin. Memories of past *posadas* made Pedro eager for this one!

When Pedro turned the corner, he shivered. Even his daydreams couldn't keep him warm. "Should have worn my winter coat," he said, shoving his hands deep into his pockets and turtling his neck deep into his collar.

Pedro decided to take the shortcut down Naranja Street, even though Mama had said she wished he wouldn't. That was where the indigents lived, camped on the corners. Pedro wondered why Mama didn't just call them homeless people like they were instead of a fancy name.

He tried to walk past, but his eyes saw anyway. They were all there, bundled up as best they could. Stan the Man, the Vietnam veteran who always wore a camouflage jacket and a blue bandanna. Gypsy June, jangling away with her layers of skirts and what must be a hundred bangle bracelets. The man they called The Elm, propped against the wall. Pedro wondered if his real name was Elmer or Elmo or if folks nicknamed him that because he was stiff and rooted as a tree. There were several others, but those were the famous ones, the ones everyone knew.

Pedro's footsteps finally left them behind, but their faces stayed with him. He dashed up the steps to school. Its warmth welcomed him like a hug.

During the day, Pedro looked out as huge wet snowflakes splotched the windows. Some of them seemed to turn into faces, like those of the people on Naranja Street. Pedro shivered, just thinking about going home in his jacket. Then he thought, *At least I have a home to go to.*

After school, Pedro closed his eyes against the driving storm and heard Mama's horn. He ducked into the car and hugged his arms to his chest. "Th-thanks, M-mama." His teeth chattered.

Mama smiled. "I thought a *posada* shopper might appreciate a lift."

Mama drove slowly, slowly through the snowy city. Past City Hall. Past Lincoln Park. Past Fine Arts Dance Academy. Down Naranja Street.

Pedro pressed his face to the glass. Gypsy June and Stan the Man and four other folks were gathered around a smoking can, rubbing their hands and rocking from one foot to another. Someone had covered The Elm with a blanket.

The car left the homeless folks behind, but their faces followed Pedro.

The festive Mexican market tickled all of Pedro's senses. Clay nativity figurines sat on display tables. Aromas of foods mingled tantalizingly together. Brightly colored streamers snaked around door-ways and columns. Music flowed from speakers, and windchimes tinkled from any movement. Piñatas of every size and shape danced, pranced, and pirouetted from their ceiling hooks.

Pedro spotted an owl piñata right away. Its wide, staring eyes reminded him of The Elm. "That's the one," he said.

"Don't you want to look closer at the other ones?" Mama asked.

"No." Pedro was firm. "I like his look. He's wise."

Pedro and Mama filled a basket with sweets and treats and took them and the piñata home. Papa helped them unload the car. "All set," Mama said. "Now all we have to do is wait for the day."

Pedro took the shortcut to school every day whether he wore his winter coat or not. Gypsy June yelled out, "You're gettin' to be a regular 'round here." Pedro said nothing.

Stan the Man walked up and said, "Good of you to come by, School Boy." Now he had a nickname, too. *Don't talk to strangers*, Pedro reminded himself.

The days crept closer to *posada* night. School had been out for two days already. Last night it had snowed again. Pedro wondered if the can was smoking on Naranja Street and if The Elm's blanket was warm and dry.

Pedro stuffed the piñata and closed it up again. Mama and Papa dusted tables, mixed punch, and set out bowls and candles.

Right before the guests arrived, Mama felt Pedro's forehead. "Are you ill?"

"You're not acting like yourself." Papa had noticed, too.

Pedro flushed. "I can't do it," he said. "I can't have a party in a warm cozy house while people are shivering and hungry right down the street."

Mama threw her hands up. "I have asked you not to go that way, Pedro. You shouldn't be seeing things like that."

"But I did, Mama. I saw them. And I see their faces all the time in my mind even when I'm not looking at them."

Papa said, "You're too young to be worried about such problems. Now your guests will be here any second. Cheer up, son. Where's your fiesta face?" He touched Pedro under the chin.

For a moment, no one said a thing. Pedro thought his ears would explode from the silence. Did he dare contradict his parents? He glanced at the wise owl piñata. It seemed to wink at him.

"I am old enough to pick out my own piñata and fill it . . ." Pedro gulped. " . . . and to share it with anyone I want. And that's what I'm going to do."

Pedro got a chair and took down the piñata. He thought his arms would break from the weight. Suddenly Papa's strong arms were under it, too, and it felt as light as air again.

The guests were singing the pilgrim song outside the door, begging to be let in. Papa opened it while Mama pulled on her coat.

The guests were surprised. Little Aleta said, "No fair. You didn't even say, 'There's no room here,' yet."

Papa held up his hands. "Keep your coats on, everyone. Pedro will explain."

Never had there been such a procession down Naranja Street before! Pilgrims of every size and age toted food and gifts. Steam rose from foiled bowls. Candle flames left white trails in the calm, cold night. Papa and Pedro pulled the huge owl along on a sled.

Gypsy June saw them first. "Bless my soul," she exclaimed. "The cold must be makin' my eyes see mirages."

Stan the Man looked up. "That's no mirage. That's School Boy come to visit," he said, "and a whole heavenly host besides!"

Pedro looked at The Elm. He lifted his head, and his smile lit up his face.

"This is all upside down and backward," Pedro's cousin Alberto laughed. "I never heard of a *posada* where the pilgrims go outside instead of inside!"

"A topsy-turvy tradition," Mama said, putting her arm around Pedro's shoulders.

The *posada* revved up and wound down at last. Pedro went to bed thinking of Gypsy June and Stan the Man and The Elm. He could still see the lights dancing in their eyes, even after his own were closed.